LITTLE TOOT
on the
GRAND CANAL

LITTLE TOOT

on the
GRAND CANAL

by HARDIE GRAMATKY —

G.P. PUTNAM'S SONS   NEW YORK

To Andrew Prentice Smith

E

c.1 8

Other books by Hardie Gramatky:
LITTLE TOOT
HERCULES
LOOPY
CREEPER'S JEEP
SPARKY
HOMER AND THE CIRCUS TRAIN
BOLIVAR
NIKOS AND THE SEA GOD
LITTLE TOOT ON THE THAMES

Little Toot loved life on the river. He tooted and towed with the hardworking tugboats. He did figure 8's on the river. And at times the little tugboat went on adventures around old docks and wharves.

He always liked to explore.

One day his father, Big Toot, took him on a real adventure. Together they went to Venice, a land far over the sea. Big Toot is the mightiest tugboat on the ocean, so Little Toot had nothing to fear.

When they got to Venice, Big Toot had work to do in the shipyard. And Little Toot was left all alone. Big round smoke balls welled up out of his smokestack and he tried hard to hold back a tear. Little Toot was afraid.

But not for long. He began to see
and hear Venice. It was beautiful!
Bells rang. Bands played. It looked
like a carnival of fun.

Little Toot bounded across the bay.

Venice, indeed, was a lovely place.

In front was a palace of pink and white marble. It looked like a jewel box open to the sea. Beyond that was a golden cathedral. And a tall bell tower chimed out gay tunes.

Yet with all this gaiety there was a sad note. The sad note came from the singing gondoliers. It was not that the gondoliers were unhappy. Not at all. They had nothing at all to be unhappy about, yet the songs they sang were sad.

But Little Toot was in no mood for sad songs. And especially not today. Today he was out to have fun.

By a stroke of good luck a high tide washed him into the Piazza of San Marco and past the golden cathedral. Great jeweled domes sparkled in the sunlight and frescoes flashed like fire.

So exciting was it that it sparked a spirit of adventure in Little Toot he had never quite known before.

Then even more exciting, out he came into the Grand Canal. Magnificent mansions rose on all sides like palaces of princes and kings. Most magnificent of all was a house on the canal that looked like a birthday cake. Its doorways and windows were trimmed with pink frosting and icing dripped down into the canal. Even its fine-lace balconies were made of spun sugar.

This was gorgeous enough, yet even more to Little Toot's taste was a forest of candystick canes that grew right out of the canal. They were delicious-looking, red and white striped candystick canes... the most beautiful thing he had seen in all Venice.

Now Little Toot was really happy.

So happy was he, he could have stayed there forever. He may well have, too, had he not taken a wrong turn. It was the worst turn he could have taken, because it took him down into a darkened canal.

Suddenly before him he saw the Bridge of Sighs.

It was an awful thing for a little tugboat to see. The bridge looked like a monster that had turned into stone. And it grew out of a prison with black barred windows.

Great round smoke balls welled out of little Toot's smokestack. He was filled with such fear he didn't know which way to turn.

He wanted his father. More than anything else he wanted to go home.

He dashed for the lagoon.
But just then the bells of
San Marco began to ring.
And all the birds flew into
the air.

When the birds saw the unhappy little tugboat, they all flew down again. They fluttered their wings around him like worried friends wringing their hands.

No one can be unhappy in Venice. The old saying is true. In no time at all the Bridge of Sighs was forgotten.

Little Toot and the birds became companions from the beginning. They loved to have fun and play games. Soon they were racing down narrow canals and squeezing under all the low bridges.

The day was so beautiful. Bells rang. Bands played. And, as though they had always been waiting for this . . . shopkeepers, waiters, and bootblacks alike . . . everyone joined in the fun.

Even the great bronze
horses high on the balcony of
San Marco pranced with the
joy of the crowd.

But nothing could be done to change the spirit of the singing gondoliers.

Their songs grew sadder than before.

No one took notice of them and all went on with their fun.

In a game of hide-and-seek Little Toot found a friendly-looking building with a painting on its front. Its water door was open, so he ducked right in.

But it wasn't the friendly place he had hoped for. Fire poured from a furnace, filling the place with fumes. Hot melting glass boiled over in black caldrons. It was the shop of the glassblower.

Before the poor little tugboat could find his way out again, he inhaled hot molten glass down into his smokestack.

It burned awfully! Out he came, coughing and choking. He tried to blow smoke balls, but none would come out. Harder, he tried . . . then even harder.

Suddenly, and as if by magic, instead of his big black smoke balls, out came *bubbles of glass.*

It was enough to humiliate anyone. To make matters worse, there were the *carabinieri*. They popped out from behind everything. The carabinieri are the police. They protect Venice from pirates.

There had not been pirates around for years, still the carabinieri were on guard. With nothing better to do for the moment, they decided to put the little tugboat in chains.

Suddenly, the boom of a cannon halted everything. A pirate ship had entered the harbor unnoticed. Already it had anchored right in the lagoon.

Then quickly over the sides came pirates bulging with pistols. Quicker still, they overpowered the carabinieri.

The pirates lost no time in looting. They stole rubies and emeralds from the cathedral and pearls from the pink and white palace. The scoundrels had no shame.

In no time at all their pockets were stuffed with precious jewels and their eyes were filled with greed.

Indeed, they were so greedy they tore the wings off the golden lion.

And what was even worse, they ripped the spun-sugar balcony off the house that looked like a birthday cake.

But when the pirates came to the candystick canes, they had gone just too far. Little Toot set up an awful howl. Those were his favorite red-and-white striped candystick canes . . . the most valued treasure in all Venice.

Without help from anyone he took on the pirates single-handed. He darted in and out like a mother bird, trying desperately to draw the pirates away from his candystick canes.

It was no use. The hoodlums only laughed at the little tugboat. And to get rid of him they drove him back into the shop of the glassblower.

What a sad day for Venice. All their beautiful treasures were aboard the pirate ship.

Never again would bells ring. Never more would the birds fly so happily.

Even the sad singing gondoliers now had reason to be sad.

But Little Toot was not ready to give up. Without anyone noticing, he slipped out of the shop of the glassblower. He coughed and choked as before, and again he was blowing glass bubbles.

This time, though, instead of blowing ordinary glass bubbles, he blew bubbles of richly colored, beautiful Venetian glass.

So dazzling were the bubbles they sparkled in the sunlight like enormous jewels.

When the pirates saw them they stopped and stared. This was a prize too tempting to resist. And almost too much for their large, greedy eyes.

They dropped everything they had stolen and raced after the great giant pearls.

Like a swarm of bees they pursued the bubbles through all the byways of Venice.

Then, they chased the bubbles through the courtyard of the pink and white palace and up the great marble stairs.

But those foolish pirates!
They pushed to be first over
the Bridge of Sighs. Then
they fought their way wildly
into prison.

When iron gates of the dungeon clanged shut behind them, all the bells in Venice began to ring. Bands played. And happy birds flew into the air.

Happiest of all were the gondoliers. Their celebration on the Grand Canal was without equal. And the songs they sang were so joyous, everyone sang along with them.

And the carabinieri joined in with the chorus.

Presents of silver and gold were offered to Little Toot. But politely and with a smile he refused.

If the truth were known, the little tugboat would have been happy with a candystick cane. But then, no one thought even to ask him.

Happily, someone did.